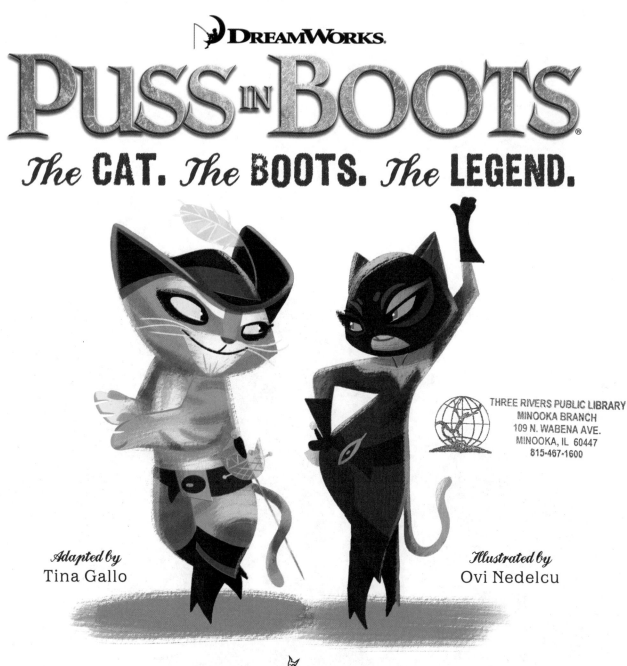

DREAMWORKS.

PUSS IN BOOTS.

The CAT. The BOOTS. The LEGEND.

Adapted by
Tina Gallo

Illustrated by
Ovi Nedelcu

SIMON SPOTLIGHT
New York London Toronto Sydney New Delhi

SIMON SPOTLIGHT
An imprint of Simon & Schuster Children's Publishing Division
1230 Avenue of the Americas, New York, New York 10020
Puss In Boots ® & © 2011 DreamWorks Animation L.L.C. All rights reserved.
All rights reserved, including the right of reproduction in whole or in part in any form.
SIMON SPOTLIGHT and colophon are registered trademarks of Simon & Schuster, Inc.
For information about special discounts for bulk purchases, please contact
Simon & Schuster Special Sales at 1-866-506-1949 or business@simonandschuster.com.
Manufactured in the United States of America 0911 LAK
1 2 3 4 5 6 7 8 9 10   First Edition
ISBN 978-1-4424-2996-3
ISBN 978-1-4424-3939-9 (eBook)

When I was a kitten, I was discovered on the steps of the San Ricardo orphanage where I met a large, egg-shaped boy named Humpty Alexander Dumpty. Humpty told me he dreamed of finding magic beans. He said the beans would grow into a vine that would rise into the clouds. There a fearsome Giant lived in a castle with a Golden Goose who laid golden eggs.

I told Humpty I wanted to be a part of his dream. From that day on, we weren't just friends—we were brothers.

As teenagers, Humpty and I looked for trouble. One day, we were throwing rocks off a rooftop when one of them hit the door of a carriage, causing it to swing open. A bull came charging out of the carriage toward an old woman crossing the street. I reacted on instinct and saved the woman. She turned out to be the Comandante's mother.

For my bravery I was given a hat, a sword, and a pair of boots. It was an odd gift for a cat, but I looked *good*. One moment had changed my life. The world opened up to me, and I vowed never to steal again.

While the light of my path grew brighter, Humpty's road grew ever
darker. He tricked me into helping him rob the Bank of San Ricardo.
But the police found us, and they chased us all the way to the town bridge.

On the bridge, our carriage hit a stone pillar and it flew over the edge.
The money Humpty had stolen was lost forever.

Humpty had fallen down, and he could not get up.
"Puss, save me!" he pleaded as the police arrived.
Humpty had betrayed me, so I saved myself instead. Humpty
was caught and sent to jail. That day I lost my home, my
honor, and my brother—and I became an outlaw.

I longed to return to San Ricardo and repay my debt. One night, years later, I heard some men say that two thieves named Jack and Jill had found the magic beans of legend. If I could get my hands on the magic beans, I could repay my debt and leave my life of crime forever.

I tracked Jack and Jill down at an old hotel. They had a lockbox containing the magic beans. I could have easily stolen the beans and been on my way, but another cat crossed my path. We were discovered by the thieves, and I barely made it out of the hotel alive.

I chased this strange cat down the street and into a cantina. I was ready to fight, but the mystery cat challenged me to a dance-off! We danced the Flamenco, the Litter Box, and the Worms—and matched each other move for move. Then it got ugly. I whacked my opponent over the head with a guitar. He yelled and tore off his mask. But he was a *she*!

"*Señorita*, wait! Let me buy you some *leche*!" I called out, following her into a back room.

Suddenly I smelled something breakfasty. And there was Humpty.

Humpty had figured out how to get the magic beans that would take him to the Giant's castle. And my dance foe—Kitty Softpaws—was his partner. A master thief, Kitty was not as good as they said. She was *better*. Still, Humpty needed my help.

At first I refused. But then I thought about paying back San Ricardo for the money that was lost so long ago. So I agreed.

First we had to steal the magic beans from Jack and Jill. They were driving their wagon through Dead Man's Pass when Kitty and I quietly jumped onto the roof and climbed inside. While Jack argued with Jill, Kitty slipped the beans out of Jack's hand.

Humpty, who was following behind in his stagecoach, rode up next to the wagon so we could make our getaway. But Jack and Jill discovered us.

Jack and Jill were hot on our trail when we came to a deadly drop. Kitty and I screamed at Humpty to stop the stagecoach. I thought it was the end. Then he pulled a lever, and we took flight!

"Giant's castle, here we come!" Humpty cried.

We found the perfect place and planted the magic beans. *KABOOM!*
The ground shook, and Kitty, Humpty, and I shot up into the air on a giant
beanstalk.

Soon we were playing in the clouds! Kitty and I chased each other. Humpty stuck his face right through a cloud, and his face got covered in white fluff.

"Somewhere down there," Humpty began, "are two little kids, and they're lying on a hill staring at the clouds, dreaming about the future. That was me and you, Puss."

Soon we spotted the Giant's castle, but it was dusty and disheveled, as if no one lived there. As we got closer to the Golden Goose, we heard angry screams. I was prepared to fight the Giant—but he was long gone. The screams were coming from the Great Terror!

We tried to take the golden eggs and run, but they were too heavy. With the Great Terror fast approaching, Humpty came up with Plan B. We could take the Golden Goose. Then we'd have all the golden eggs we wanted.

We fashioned a zip line and swung across the moat surrounding the Golden Goose's jungle. The Great Terror was on our heels the entire way, but we finally made our escape with the Golden Goose.

That night we celebrated by a campfire, and everything felt right again. Now I could return home and repay my debt. I told Kitty she had my heart, and she said she liked me, too.

I thought all my troubles were over until I felt a harsh blow to my head.

The next morning I awoke completely alone. But I recognized Jack and Jill's footprints! I followed their tracks back to San Ricardo. That's when I realized Humpty had betrayed me again.

Humpty told the Comandante that I was to blame for the bank robbery. I was thrown into jail. Humpty offered the Golden Goose to the people of San Ricardo to repay the money they had lost. The town thought *he* was the hero.

In jail I learned that Humpty had been plotting his revenge since he was locked up for the bank robbery years ago. This was all part of his master plan. The next day I received another surprise—a visit from Kitty! She told me that she was sorry, and then she helped me escape from jail.

I discovered that the Great Terror was the Goose's mother. I had to save the town from destruction. The first thing I did was find Humpty.

"Get the baby over the bridge!" I told Humpty. "I'll get the mother to follow!"

Humpty drove the Golden Goose toward the town bridge in his carriage, while I led the Great Terror after her baby. As we sped toward the bridge, the carriage slammed into the edge, and the bridge started to crumble. The Great Terror fell over the side, plummeting into the water below.

Humpty and the Golden Goose also flew off the edge of the bridge. Quickly, I grabbed the rope that held them as they dangled over the abyss. But they were too heavy. I could not save them both.

Humpty did not let me choose who to save. "You have to get the Goose back to its mother. It's the only way to save San Ricardo."

Then he let go.

I pulled the Golden Goose up and gave the baby back to her mother. Then I leaned over to look for Humpty. His shell had shattered, and underneath it he was made entirely of gold! Humpty seemed happy, truly happy for the first time.

The Great Terror plucked Humpty off the ground and sailed off with him into the sky.

"I'm finally going home!" he cried.

As for me, I said good-bye to Humpty and to San Ricardo. But I did not say good-bye to Kitty. I promised her we would meet again soon.

"Sooner than you think," she told me.

That is when I noticed she had stolen my boots. Oh, she is a bad kitty!